The Lost Diary of
Erik Bloodaxe,
Viking Warrior

Another Lost Diary recently discovered

The Lost Diary of
Tutankhamun's Mummy

The Lost Diary of Erik Bloodaxe, Viking Warrior

Also known as King of Norway, King of the Hebrides, and King of the Kingdom of York

Found by
Steve Barlow and Steve Skidmore

MESSAGE TO READERS

Archaeologists excavating a barrow* on Steinmore in County
Durham, England, discovered a number of cured animal hides
covered in runes, the form of writing used by the Vikings.

F	U	TH	A	R	K	H	N	I	A	S	T	B	M	L	R
ᚠ	ᚢ	ᚦ	ᚨ	ᚱ	ᚴ	ᚼ	ᚾ	ᛁ	ᛏ	ᚾ	ᛏ	ᛒ	ᛘ	ᛚ	ᚴ

The first hide read:

ᛁᛏᚾ ᚱᚨᛁᛏ ᛏᚾ ᚾᚢᚾᚨᚱ

The hides were sent to Professor Lotta Lyes, a Norwegian expert on
Viking times. Her initial examination of the runes filled historians
with excitement. She concluded that the runes had been written in the
tenth century and contained intimate details about the private life of
Erik Bloodaxe, one of the greatest Viking warriors of all time.

It soon became clear that these incredible documents were
actually a journal written by a man previously unknown in history:
Erik's chief poet, Gorblime Leifitoutsson.

The hides have been authenticated by Yur Mustbejokinsson, a
scholar of Viking comics at the University of the North Pole.

The discoverers of the hides, Steve Barlow and Steve Skidmore,
were the obvious choices to undertake the first translation into
English of this important work. They have selected the most
interesting of the journal entries and newspaper clippings for
publication to reveal astonishing details about what life (and death)
was really like at the time of Erik Bloodaxe, king and Viking warrior.

Barrow—Viking burial mound

I, Erik Bloodaxe, Viking Prince of Norway, do hereby appoint Gorblime Leifitoutsson as my court poet, to record a full and accurate account of my triumphs and the glories of my reign.

Signed Erik

His Mark

X

I'll tell it the way it is, Erik. You won't be able to read it anyway!

If this book should dare to roam,
Box it up and send it home

TO:

~~The Royal Palace, Hordaland, Norway~~

~~Dunrulin, Orkneys~~

~~Cunerik, Jorvik~~

~~Dunrulin, Orkneys~~

~~The Old Roman Palace, Jorvik~~

~~Dunrulin, Orkneys~~

~~King's Garth, Orkneys~~

The Old Roman Palace, Jorvik

Norway

Prince Erik—sorry, King Erik now that his father's kicked the bucket—told me this morning that:

   a) since I was the only one who could read and write around here, he was appointing me as his new Skald*, and

   b) if I didn't write a praise poem to celebrate his becoming king by lunchtime he'd chop me into meaty chunks.

   So I got started and wrote:

Bright shone the sun on that spring morning,
Happy with song, the hearts of the household...

Actually, it's a terrible day! It's pouring with rain, the wind is howling, and it's freezing cold—as usual. That's Scandinavian weather for you. Everybody's miserable, but it's more than my job's worth to tell the truth. The weather is supposed to be wonderful when a new king is crowned, as an omen of a glorious reign, so we poets have to make sure that it *is* wonderful—in poems, anyway.

   I cut this article out of the paper as a souvenir:

*Skald—court poet

THE NORSE OF THE WORLD

HARALD OFF TO VALHALLA

Harald Finehair, King of Norway, died today after a long illness. The new King of Norway will be his twenty-year-old son, Erik. Harald promised Erik the throne only last week, when he placed him on the high seat and told him he was **me!** heir to the whole kingdom. This isn't going to please Erik's brothers. Harald had nine sons. Prince Olaf and Prince Sigurd both want to be king, and even nine-year-old Prince Hakon, who is currently living in England at the court of King Athelstan, thinks he should be the next prince on the throne. However, Erik is next in line to the Norwegian throne, so he's the new king.

A palace spokesperson told our reporter that the new king is good at fighting and loves raiding, looting, stealing, killing, and drinking heavily.

It sounds as though Erik is going to make a good Viking king!

DOES NORWAY NEED A KING AT ALL? See Readers' Comments p. 6

A DAY WITH THE STARS OF NORSE IMPROVEMENT See p. 9

My next official
court job was to
write a funeral poem
about King Harald. I
threw one together
pretty quickly and
read it to Erik:

There once was a king called Harald,
Who wasn't the slightest bit bald.
Vikings would stare
At his mop of Finehair,
Which kept his head safe from the cold.

Erik gave me a dirty look. "Is that the best you
can come up with?" he asked.

I said I'd do a little more work on it.

Erik said, "I'd do a lot more work on it if I
were you."

Great, I thought. Here's a guy who can't even
write his own name, and he thinks he can tell me
how to write poetry. I'd tell him to get a life, but
I don't want to end up as dog food.

We said farewell to Harald in the good old Viking way. The King's longship was dragged ashore, and wood was piled all around it. Then we laid Harald in the ship with all his possessions: his weapons and pots and pans. We even put his combs in so he'll be able to fix his hair in the next world!

Then his horse and dog were killed and laid beside him. We also put Harald's slave in the boat. The slave wasn't too happy about it, but he stopped complaining when he was killed too.

I read the new praise poem I'd written about how Harald became king by chopping up all the chieftains who didn't agree with him at the battle of Hafrsfjord:

Harald and his heroes held up their hands,
Bright shone their swords, brain-biters;
Fearful, their foes fretted and fumbled,
Great was the battle that terrible day;
Vikings victorious once again...

While I was reading, I saw King Erik wipe away a tear. *He really loved his old man*, I thought.

After my poem, a Viking warrior with no clothes on leaped out of the crowd and set fire to the wood. (Probably a good idea not to wear any clothes when you're lighting a fire.) Then we all watched as Harald went up in flames to the next world while we sang the Viking national anthem:

My Vikings 'tis of thee,
Great Vikings strong and free,
Of thee I sing!
Standing firm side by side,
Warriors who fight with pride.
From every mountainside,
Let's hail Vi-kings!

Norway

King Erik sent for me this morning and told me that we're going on a Viking raid. We are sailing on a ship called the *Wrath of Odin*. All Viking longships have names like *Wrath of Odin* or *Vengeance of Thor* or *Death Dragon*. If you're going to leap ashore in a battle fury and destroy cities, you don't want to be doing it from boats called *The Skylark* or *Bluebell*.

I asked the king what I needed to take on the trip, and he gave me a letter for my parents.

Dear Parents

A VIKING RAID

As part of the New Viking Curriculum, we are
required to develop the educational experiences
of Viking warriors. Your son has been selected to
practice his fighting skills on our Viking raid
to the Baltic Sea.

There will be plenty of opportunities for
educational plunder, and it is hoped that
your son will join in all such activities.

It must be stressed that bad behavior on such
trips is important for the reputation of Vikings
everywhere. If your son is not violent enough, he
will be sent home and not allowed to participate
in any more raids. He will also be taunted by
his classmates for being a wimp.

Depart: Dawn, from the jetty at Oslofjord
Return: For those still alive after the raid, we
hope to arrive back home in about six months.

Things to bring
Chain mail
Iron helmet (if you can afford one)
Leather tunic
Boots (real Viking boots; no hightops, please!)
Cloak
Mittens or gloves
Spare pants (in case the ones you're wearing get
dirty)
Chest to put all of the above in (and to sit on
in the ship while rowing)

Axe
Knife
Ash wood spear
Double-edged sword
Large round shield
Bow and arrows
Cooking utensils

Lunch (dried or smoked fish, smoked walrus meat, cheese, bread, etc.)
Water
Comb
Spending money (although there will be opportunities to seize money, slaves, and souvenirs from the places we raid)

Please make sure to label all items so they are easily identifiable. THIS IS IMPORTANT! If your son dies in battle, and his clothes are not properly labeled, we may not know who he is.

Sincerely,
Erik

PS: No girls allowed. They must stay at home and tend the farms while the men are away.

Tear off and return this portion

We give permission for _____ to go on the above trip. We understand that he must be healthy and strong. We also relieve the King of all responsibility in case our son gets killed while plundering and pillaging.

_____
Signature(s)   Date

It'll all end badly. mark my words.

The Dvina River, Russia

It's cold enough to freeze a walrus's tusks off, but otherwise it hasn't been a bad voyage. We've sailed up the north coast of Norway and around to the Barents Sea. There hasn't been much wind, so we've had to row most of the way, but at least rowing keeps you warm. We're now moving up the Dvina River to find someone to trade with. Of course, if Erik finds someone who doesn't want to trade, being a Viking he'll just kill him and take his stuff instead. This can cause a lot of trouble, but Vikings like trouble.

Permina

The first place we stopped was Permina. Sure enough, the people of Permina didn't want to trade.

> *High were our hearts as we stormed the great city.*
> *Thousands we slew, with savage slaughter.*
> *Permina's treasures were ours for the taking...*

Actually, Permina is a very small trading post, and Erik's warriors found only a few unlucky merchants and slaves who were too slow to get away. But Erik still made me compose a praise song for this great victory. I was trying to find a rhyme for "Aaaaargh!" when he came over to me and announced that, since he'd won a battle and was now a real Viking with a praise song and everything, he should have a nickname.

He sat playing with his axe and said he wanted to be called something like Erik the Brave or Erik Manslayer or Erik Ironfist.

Suddenly he yelled out, "Ow!" The axe had slipped and cut his finger. A drop of blood

dribbled down the axe blade.

Stupid man, I thought. But it gave me an idea…

"How about Erik Bloodaxe?" I asked.

A big grin spread over his face. "I like it, Gorblime," he said. "It's perfect!"

Denmark

We've stopped at Denmark. King Gorm the Old invited us up to his longhouse and told us to put on our best clothes because he was giving a feast in our honor.

I've been to worse parties. Here's the menu:

KING GORM'S FEAST
A LA CART MENU

They needed a cart to get all the stuff over from the Kitchen.

FIRST COURSE
Cows
Sheep
Deer
Wild boar
Veal stew
Whale stew
Seagulls
Seal
Salted fish
Fish soup
Cabbage
Peas
Onions
Seaweed
Bread

SECOND COURSE
Same as the first

THIRD COURSE
Same as the second

DRINKS
French wine (only for the chieftains)
Beer
Mead
Wild fruit juice
More beer
More mead
Even more beer
Even more mead

Drink made from honey.

Does it make you sick?

Do bees buzz in the woods?

The women did the serving, of course. A few of the Vikings got carried away, and one of them got fresh with a serving maid. You don't do that to a Viking woman unless you want your arm chopped off. The poor guy had to carry his hand home in a bag.

I'm sure I would have enjoyed myself if I didn't have a drinking problem. Every time I put my drinking horn up to my lips, *splash!*, my mead is all over my face. I've tried every horn I can find (including Erik's). Why can't someone invent a container that's easy to drink from?

During the feast, Erik told me to recite my latest poem. I had to say it from memory, and by this time my memory wasn't too good, so I just made up the parts I couldn't recall.

Food, glorious food,
Cold walrus and seagull.
Food, fabulous food,
I eat till I get ill.
Drinking and feasting lots,
I'm a Viking.
Mead, wine, and beer in pots
I'm a-liking.
Food, glorious food,
Pigs, chicken, and veal stew.
Food, glorious food,
I eat until I spew...

What a pile of garbage! Luckily, no one was listening.

Later in the evening, I noticed Erik was eyeing one of Gorm's daughters, Gunnhild. He just sat looking at her and playing with his food, and he couldn't have drunk more than a couple of gallons of beer all night. *Oh dear,* I thought, *wedding horns are in the air. He'll be sorry before he's much older.*

Sure enough, Erik popped the question the next night, and Gunnhild said yes immediately. I wouldn't like being called Mrs. Bloodaxe myself, but she gets to be queen so I guess she thinks it's worth it.

Norway

We spent all last winter with old King Gorm. When we arrived back in Norway, Erik got quite a shock. While he was away, two of his brothers had decided to take over the throne. Olaf had declared himself King of Oslofjord, and Sigurd had taken the throne of Trondlag.

Erik didn't want to make war on his own brothers, but Gunnhild threw a fit as soon as she heard. She told Erik that when she married a king called Bloodaxe she hadn't expected him to stay at home and milk the goats when people started taking over his kingdom. So then, of course, Erik had to fight. We can see who wears the fur-lined breeks* around here, can't we?

*Breeks—trousers

Tonsberg

We found Sigurd's fleet at anchor in Oslofjord near Tonsberg. He'd decided to join forces with Olaf.

> *Battle was joined, and our swords*
> *sang in greeting.*
> *Broken were spears and shields at*
> *that meeting.*
> *Many men died on that terrible day...*

Stirring stuff, isn't it? I'm getting better at this poetry.

Actually, the Battle of Tonsberg was a typical Viking fight. There's not much of a plan to Viking battles—everybody just starts warring with everybody else, and whoever's left standing wins. This time, Erik won. Olaf and Sigurd didn't, so we buried them and came home.

Fjor

Fjord Aerostä

Fjord Taurus

Fjord Explorer

CÄRÄVÄN

Tonsberg ✂

HÖNDA

Oslofjord →

NÖRSSÄ

Island of Atley

Scort

VÖLVO

MÄZDA

dheim

JÄGUAR

ROLLS RÖICE

LÄXUS

MAP of VIKING
NORWAY
N

The NORSE of the WORLD

THOR IN HOT WATER!

Last week at the Thing*, the family of Sven Yursmiling claimed that Thor Thumb had killed Sven during an argument about fishing rights. Thor denied all knowledge of the murder and claimed he was being set up.

King Erik, listening to the evidence, said that Thor could prove his innocence in two ways:

1) by putting his hand in boiling water, or

2) by walking on red-hot iron.

If Thor's wound healed quickly, it would prove that Thor didn't kill Sven, and he could go free.

Brave boy Thor took the plunge and chose the boiling-water test.

*Thing—a council of justice

OUCH!

He thrust his hand into a huge pot of boiling water. Apart from going cross-eyed, crying, hopping up and down, and then shouting out, "By Odin, that's warm!" Thor took it very well.

When he pulled his arm from the pot, blisters already reddened his skin.

There was a roar of laughter in the Thing as King Erik joked that Thor looked as if he had a Thor arm. Thor didn't laugh.

STOP THE PRESSES!

News just in: *A week after his trial, Thor's arm has not healed. King Erik decided that Thor was guilty and exiled him for three years.*

Civil liberties groups say the boiling-water treatment is cruel, but judges argue that it is an effective deterrent. What's your opinion? Call our special hotline number.

Noggin The Nog Wins Medal in Spear Toss
See p. 4

Ask Ann Landersson
See p. 8

AD 932

Island of Atley, Norway

King Erik and Queen Gunnhild decided to pay a
visit to a steward of theirs named Bard on the
Island of Atley. I tagged along for the voyage.

When we got there, Bard was already
entertaining some other guests. Gunnhild was
pretty miffed.

"And just who is more important than the King
and Queen?" she asked nastily.

The other guests were Egil Skallagrimson
and his men, it turned out.

Gunnhild erupted like a volcano! Didn't Bard
know there was a blood feud between Egil's
family and the King's? Wasn't he aware that Erik's
dad had sent Egil's dad into exile in Iceland, along
with Egil himself and his brother, Thorolf?

This was true. What Gunnhild didn't mention
was that Erik later begged his dad to let Egil and
Thorolf come back after they had given Erik his
first longship. I wondered if I should remind
Gunnhild of this, but I decided not to say
anything after I noticed the look in her eye.

There wasn't much Gunnhild could do except grumble, and since Egil had arrived first, Erik couldn't really throw him out. I'll bet Bard had some explaining to do. Better him than me.

We all sat down to a feast together this evening.
It wasn't what you'd call friendly. The hall was
full of suspicious glares and hidden weapons. Just
one wrong word would have started a fight.

When Bard brought the ale out, Egil's men
began to mutter. It turned out that Bard had told
them he'd run out of ale, and all they'd been given
to drink since they arrived was sour milk.

We started drinking the ale, and soon Egil's
men were rowdy. Egil stood on the table and
made up an insulting poem about Bard:

> *He said he'd no ale,*
> *For me and the guys:*
> *For Bard is a meanie*
> *And tells big fat lies...*

Bard told him to sit down and behave. The next thing we knew he had Egil's sword sticking through him. Everybody started yelling, and by the time order was restored, Egil had vanished.

Erik swore Egil would pay and commanded us all to go out and search the island until we found him.

Personally, I think the best way to search for a madman with a sharp sword is to make sure you don't find him. I wandered around shouting things like, "I think I'll look behind the cowsheds next," to give him plenty of time to get away.

We couldn't find Egil on the island. At daybreak, Erik sent ships out to search some smaller islands nearby. One of the ships didn't come back, so Erik went to look for it.

He found the crew (what was left of it) sitting on a tiny island. Erik asked them what had happened, and they all looked down and shuffled their feet.

"Well," said Erik. "What's the story?"

It turned out that Egil had escaped by swimming to this island. When Erik's men showed up he attacked them, killed three, and stole their ship. They'd been sitting there all day waiting to be rescued.

Erik ranted and raved at them, yelling things like "You call yourselves Vikings?" and "My old grandmother could have done better," but Egil had escaped and that's all there was to it.

It doesn't bother me. I think Bard deserved what he got. Taking ale away from a Viking is like trying to take meat away from a pack of wolves. But Erik is furious: he's had a loyal steward killed and one of his ships stolen—and he's been made to look foolish. I wrote a poem about it:

Brave Egil swam over the fjord
And brandished his big Viking swjord.
He started to gloat
When he stole Erik's boat,
An insult that can't be ignjored!

I haven't shown that one to Erik.

THE NORSE OF THE WORLD

GOOD TO BE BACK!

EXCLUSIVE!

Egil Skallagrimson is back in Norway!

NORSE OF THE WORLD readers will remember that mischievous Egil recently made a fool of King Erik by:

- *killing one of Erik's stewards*
- *stealing one of Erik's ships*
- *making King Erik look like a complete idiot.*

The NORSE OF THE WORLD has learned that Egil has returned from raiding in Denmark and is staying with Chieftain Thorir at his fjord-side longhouse.

NO COMMENT!

We sent a reporter to King Erik Bloodaxe to ask for his views on Egil's return. Unfortunately Erik slammed the door in our reporter's face.

From this we conclude that Erik is NOT A HAPPY CAMPER!

Longboat Race Special:

STANFJORD vs. HÄRVÄRD

See Sports Pages

Norway

There's trouble with the Queen. Erik had to send her brother, Eyvind Shabby, into exile, and it's all Gunnhild's fault.

Gunnhild heard that Egil was coming to the great spring feast, so she told Eyvind to kill him. Eyvind's always had a bad temper, probably because kids tease him. They say, "Are you Shabby?" and when he says yes they say, "Well, get some new clothes!" and run off laughing.

However, Egil's brother, Thorolf, showed up at the feast instead. When he realized that Egil wasn't coming, Eyvind got ticked off and killed one of Thorolf's men before anyone could stop him. (I guess he thought if he couldn't get Egil, killing one of his allies would be the next best thing.)

If anyone else had murdered a man at a sacred feast, Erik would have had him killed on the spot. Since Eyvind is the Queen's brother, he got off with banishment. Not that this makes Gunnhild happy. She's locked herself in her room and won't come out. She and Erik are shouting at each other through the locked door, and you can hear them all over the palace.

Egil and Thorolf have gone to England to fight for King Athelstan, which is a little odd. Vikings will fight for anyone if it pays well enough, but Athelstan's a Saxon and a sworn Viking enemy. Maybe they're trying to impress Erik's creepy little brother, Hakon.

Anyway, good riddance if you ask me. At least it'll keep them out of Erik's way.

Norway

There's trouble brewing with Egil again. He's coming back from England to claim an inheritance for his wife, Asgerd, at the Gula Assembly.* I had a little trouble explaining this to Erik.

He said, "I thought she was married to Egil's brother, Thorolf."

"She was," I told him. "But Thorolf was killed fighting in England last winter."

"So she's Thorolf's widow?"

"Yes, but she's also Egil's wife. He married her this spring."

I explained that Asgerd's sister was married to a guy named Onund, who's a good friend of Queen Gunnhild. Asgerd's father died last month, and legally she and her sister should each get half the loot. But Gunnhild is determined that her pal Onund should have it all, and she especially doesn't want Egil to have any of the money.

*Gula Assembly—the main Norwegian law court in Viking times

"That's all there is to it," I concluded. "Simple."

King Erik nodded wisely and said, "Just run that by me again, will you?"

He's got the brains of a slug. It's not all glory and riches being a court poet.

The NORSE OF THE WORLD

RIOT AT GULA!

The Gula Assembly exploded into violence today as Egil Skallagrimson's case came before the court.

Mr. Skallagrimson looked pale but determined as he guided his petite blonde wife, Asgerd (33), through the court. This was held as usual on a level stretch of ground marked out with hazel rods and holy ropes that no one is allowed to break.

When Queen Gunnhild saw the case was likely to be won by Egil, she told her brother Alf to break up the court. Alf and his men broke the rods and ropes and attacked the judges. Immediately, fighting erupted.

Following the violence, King Erik banished Alf from Norway for causing a riot in a sacred place.

Eyvind Shabby always used to do Gunnhild's dirty work, but when Erik sent him into exile, the job went to her little brother, Alf. Now Erik has had to banish Alf too, and it's all Gunnhild's fault. But guess what? Gunnhild's locked herself in her room again.

Erik hasn't told Gunnhild that Egil escaped to Iceland. He'd better not show his face around here again, or there'll be real trouble.

AD 935

Norway

Two of Erik's chieftains had a disagreement over a piece of land this week, so they challenged each other to a holmganga[1] duel. They laid a cloak on the ground and pegged it down with hazel rods. Then the referee called them together and made his announcement:

"My Lords, Warriors, Wenches, Housekarls,[2] and Thralls[3]! Introducing a super-welter-weights-of-gore contest between, on my right, Sigrid the Fat and, on my left, Harald the Slightly Chubby.

"Right, boys, I want a good clean fight. No holding, clinching, or chopping below the belt. The first one to step off the cloak is a nithing.[4]

Ready, get set, go—"

[1] Holmganga—trial by combat [2] Housekarl—a domestic servant
[3] Thrall—a slave [4] Nithing—a coward

It was a good fight. Sigrid used his axe, and Harald used his sword. Both of them had shields. They stood, swinging their weapons and trying to wound each other. The loser is usually the one with the most wounds, but it didn't turn out quite like that this time. I wrote a poem about what happened:

> Sig and Hal went up the hill
> To fight in the holmganga.
> Sig went down with a busted crown
> 'Cause Harald's sword was longa!
> But Hal was slow to parry, so
> Young Sigrid was the winner!
> He cried "By gum!" and slit Hal's tum;
> So Harald lost his dinner!

Erik left before the holmganga was over. I think that underneath that tough exterior, he's just an old softy.

The NORSE of the WORLD

ERIK'S OUT!

King Erik Bloodaxe has been booted off the throne! The King has been making himself very unpopular lately by rendering unfair judgments and raiding where he shouldn't.

A source close to the King is putting the blame on Queen Gunnhild. As our source said, "She's spent the past six years telling Erik that a king can do anything he wants to."

me — and I hope Erik doesn't find out!

The NORSE of the WORLD says, "Well, ex-King Erik, as you've just found out, you can't!"

The final straw came when Erik's brother Hakon returned from England and landed at Trondheim. Hakon, only fifteen years old, has teamed up with King Athelstan of England and Earl Sigurd of Hladir to claim the Norwegian throne. He is also supported by most of the chiefs and earls in the country.

Early reports indicated that Erik was ready to challenge them to a fight. However, his advisers have warned him that Hakon has a massive army and victory would be impossible. Erik has agreed to leave Norway tomorrow.

me again!

So, it's bye-bye, Erik, hello, Hakon!

Should Erik go?

Call the Viking Hotline to say who you want to be King:

Dial 010101000865759942341562467890754678234190987634526 for Erik and

1 for Hakon

Caution: Anybody calling for Erik will be in dead trouble . . . or just dead

Oslofjord

We sailed away from Norway forever this
morning. I composed a sorrowful song of parting:

> *We are sailing, we are sailing*
> *Down the fjord to the sea.*
> *We are sailing stormy waters*
> *To where Vikings can be free.*

We're a pretty small party; just Erik and Gunnhild,
a few faithful supporters . . . oh, and me of course.

Not many people came to see us off. Vikings
don't care who's on the throne as long as there's
lots of raiding and feasting.

There may not be much of that with Hakon in
charge, however. From what I hear, he became a
Christian at Athelstan's court, and we all know
what they're like—all that turning the other cheek
and loving one another. How's a good Viking
going to have any fun with someone like that?

The Orkney Islands

We have reached a group of bare and windswept islands, called the Orkneys, to the north of Scotland.

According to Viking custom, Erik threw the pillars of his high seat* into the sea so that the gods can lead us to our new home. We'll make our settlement at the place where the pillars drift ashore.

Our carpenter (old Knutty Pinesson) is making Erik a new set of high-seat pillars. We tried to find the old ones for a week, but Gunnhild said she wasn't going to spend the rest of her life floating around icy seas. In the end, Erik chose a bay with a stream and some flat fields for farming, and here we are. The land is brown, the sea is brown, and the sky is brown. Everything else is even less interesting to look at.

HOME SWEET HOME   *High seat – throne

These islands are the pits.

Back in Norway we make our houses out of wood, but there aren't any trees here. We're using turf laid on top of dirt and stones.

Once we landed, Erik put us to work building a long hall so everyone has a place to go in the evenings to eat and listen to me recite praise poems for Erik (as if that's anyone's idea of a good time). Even the pigs, sheep, and goats are being kept in the hall until we can build a barn for them.

I told Gunnhild that it wasn't much fun sleeping with a pig. She said no, but after all, she had married him.

We finally finished the barn, thank Odin. With so many Vikings and animals living in one room, the smell was terrible. All the animals were complaining.

Everybody has been busy building stores and

houses. We've even got a smithy so that Gotmore Muselsthanusson (a great musclebound dunce) can forge tools and weapons.

When I say everyone has been busy, I don't mean Erik, of course. Or Gunnhild. They've got thralls working for them. Erik just sits in his special chair in the longhouse bossing everyone around, and Gunnhild sits there bossing Erik. He wouldn't dare answer her back. If he did, she could ask for a divorce and get half of his property (although there's not much of that these days!).

Crops have been planted: barley, rye, oats, peas, beans, and turnips. More important, ale and mead are being brewed. We might even be able to serve a halfway decent feast one day soon.

Gunnhild is still griping about missing the Norwegian weather. I don't see why. It's just as foggy, cold, and wet here in the Orkneys as it was back home.

What have I done to deserve this?

Some of Erik's men brought their kids with them, but we forgot to bring a teacher, so guess who Erik decided would run the new school?

I made up a poem to help the kids learn the names of the gods:

Asgard, above, is where all the gods dwell.
Balder was gentle; the gods loved him well.
Cats pull the chariot in which Freyja rides,
Deep dig the Dwarves, and the Dark Elves besides.
Embla, first woman, companion to Ask,
Frigg is the wife who takes Odin to task.
Garm is the guardian who fills souls with dread,
Hel is his mistress, the queen of the dead.
Idunn grows apples that keep the gods young.
Jomungand touches his tail with his tongue!
Kvasir, the poet, wiser than wise;
Loki, the trickster, the god of disguise.
Mimir lost his head, yet his voice spoke again.
Norns know the fates and the fortunes of men.
Odin, Creator and Father of All,
Prince of Valhalla, the great heroes' hall.
Queen of the seas, and wife to Aegir,
Is Ran, whom all sailors have reason to fear.
Sif of the golden hair, married to Thor,

Thunder god, mighty Upholder of law.
Vigard shall be the last great battle plain,
When Fenrir the wolf shall break free of his chain:
And X is the clashing of swords as they meet.
No human or god shall survive the defeat;
Yggdrasil, the World Tree, once more stands alone
And Z marks the end of the world we have known.

The poem took me forever to write, and the class didn't even listen.

Kids today! I blame the parents.

AD 937

The Orkney Islands

A lot of Vikings have joined Erik's settlement here in Orkney. The raiding season has just started, so we're off to attack Scotland. I think Erik just needs an excuse to get away from Gunnhild for a while. She's been complaining about having to look after the farm while he's away—but the work has to be done, and it's the woman's place to do it. Anyway, she's got plenty of thralls to help her, and Erik's promised to bring back some duty-free jewels and perfume from the towns and monasteries we raid, so she'll just have to live with it.

Some new warriors are joining us on the trip. They're a strange bunch, but we can't be choosy—you can't get good help nowadays.

Gotno Frendsatall—
he stinks, even for a Viking.

Knut Veryclever—
he's thick as a brick but a good fighter.

Wats Upwithyousson—
I don't think he
really wants to go—
he's always crying.

Syng Usasongsson—
he thinks he can
sing, Thor help us.

Sig Asaparrot—
he gets seasick.
Not a good trait
for a Viking.

*Olaf
Ifitsfunnysson*—
he tells awful
jokes.

Ican't Swimsson—he's afraid of the water.
I don't know why Erik chose him.

We had to buy more ships from the local
boatbuilder for the raid.

KORSU KNTRUSTMEMYSSON
SHIPS LIMITED

OUR GUARANTEE TO YOU

Top-quality workmanship
All our ships are leak-free
- All sides made up of overlapping long planks of oak
- Solid pine masts
- Animal hair and moss dipped in tar to keep out water
- Iron-rivet fastening system

NO-LEAK GUARANTEE
AIR BAG PROTECTION (sails)

- All ships have top-quality unleaded woolen sails

JUST IN: NEW MODELS

HAFSKIP
- Over 75 feet (23m) long
- 16 feet (5m) wide
- Only 22 tons
- 120 miles (193km) per day!
- Ideal for shallow water

SKUTA WARSHIPS
- Hold 15 men
- Oars included
- Low-slung sides for speed
- 9 knots under sail
- 5 knots when rowed by full crew
- Ideal for a quick raid!

DREKI WARSHIPS

- Hold over 50 oarsmen!
- Any design of dragon carved into the prow
- Guaranteed to scare people and bring good luck in your raiding

KNORRS

- Top-quality trading boats
- Deeper and wider than the longboats
- Ideal for transporting cattle and cargo stolen on raids

LOWEST PRICES

Free navigation set with every two Dragon Boats.
Everything you need for navigating your way across the sea including:

- Know Your Stars for Navigation book
- A simple sun compass

Also

- Free owner's manual
- Free "My other ship's a Dragon Boat" sticker

We've been busy loading supplies on board: weapons, tools, cooking items, chests, furs, water, more weapons, and some food (although we'll try to steal as much food as we can when we start raiding).

Erik is even taking his bed. Gunnhild is furious. She told him he'd better make sure he doesn't lose it or he needn't bother coming home. Erik's sailing in a Dragon Boat—I suppose it's named after his wife.

Scotland

We sailed quietly up the river this morning, and there before us lay a small town. It looked very friendly and peaceful. Well, we couldn't have that, could we?

We ran the longships aground and crept up to the town gates. Then we charged, chanting our terrifying Viking battle cry:

> A-Viking we will go,
> A-Viking we will go!
> Hi, ho, the dairy-o,
> A-Viking we will go!

The men from the town rushed out to defend it, only to fall before us, as my praise song tells:

> *Scots scattered; wild wolves*
> *And eagles at evening surveyed the scene.*
> *Battle cranes cried over the tragic fields,*
> *As hungry ravens circled overhead...*

Oh, yes, it was a great victory. The defenders were half asleep and not many were armed, which is usually what happens when you attack people before dawn. Most of the women and children got away—we had to let them go or there'd be nobody to raid next time. We grabbed whatever we could carry, set fire to the town, and fled. It was just a routine raid, really, but I still had to write a praise song about it.

Dublin, Ireland

What a year!

The raiding down the west coast of Scotland was a waste of time. A lot of the villages had been raided already, and there's a limit to how often you can pillage a village before everything that can be stolen is gone.

So instead of going home without the duty-free stuff he'd promised Gunnhild, Erik decided to sail over to Ireland to pay a visit to old Olaf Guthfrithson. Olaf's been King of Dublin for four years now. The Vikings in Ireland are a friendly group, and we had a great time.

King Olaf was especially happy to see us. We soon found out why. He wants to recapture the Viking Kingdom of Jorvik* from the Saxons, and he's trying to raise an army.

Erik told Olaf he wouldn't mind a shot at Athelstan, since the Saxon king helped Erik's rotten brother Hakon steal the Norwegian throne. So it was agreed that when Olaf sets sail next year, Erik and the rest of us will be with him.

* Jorvik – present-day English city of York.

AD 939

The Orkney Islands

Well, it turns out that Erik isn't going to fight Athelstan after all, because Athelstan's dead. A messenger brought the news just as we were about to set sail this morning.

That should make our job a whole lot easier. The Saxons will be too busy fighting among themselves about who's going to be the next king to worry about us.

Jorvik

We sailed up the river to Jorvik this morning with not a Saxon in sight, and here we are.

I'll say one thing for Jorvik—it's big. There's nothing like it in Norway. Olaf tells me it's the biggest city in England—after London—and the richest.

As we got nearer, the walls with their eight great towers rose out of the mist. It was like sailing into Valhalla. Until, that is, we got closer to the wharves. The Romans built the walls. They also built drains, but from the smell of the place, I'd guess they stopped working long ago. The river that runs through Jorvik is called the Ouse. It should be called the Gross. Phew!

Most of the people who live in Jorvik are Danish Vikings, so when Olaf told them that he was going to be king, they all cheered like crazy because that meant a Viking would be in charge again. They came crowding down to the wharf and carried us into the city singing the Danish national anthem:

There is nothing like a Dane,
Nothing in the world!
There is nothing you can name
That is anything like a Dane...

Olaf's now planning to capture the Danelaw, part of England that the old Saxon king Alfred gave to the Danes when it looked as if we Vikings were going to take over the whole country. We would have, too, if Alfred hadn't burned those cakes (don't ask how he managed to beat us by burning cakes—it's a long story). So we agreed to leave him alone if he let Vikings rule the Danelaw.

But a couple of years ago, Olaf got trounced by Athelstan at the Battle of Brunanburgh, and the Saxons have moved back into the Danelaw. There goes the neighborhood.

So now Olaf wants the Saxons out. Erik agrees, and he's looking forward to a great battle with the Saxons. I can't wait.

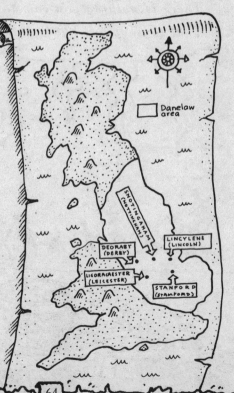

Danelaw area

SNOTINGAHAM (NOTTINGHAM)

LINCYLENE (LINCOLN)

DEORABY (DERBY)

LIGORACAESTER (LEICESTER)

STANFORD (STAMFORD)

Ligoracaester

The campaign to recapture
the Danelaw was the most
boring war I've ever fought.
Before we'd got to Lincylene,
all the troops were chanting
"Ea-sy, ea-sy, ea-sy!"
and it was.

"Ea-sy,
Ea-sy,
Ea-sy!"

King Edmund* (Athelstan's brother) had
gathered an army by the time we reached
Ligoracaester, and we thought there'd be some
action at last. Unfortunately, Wulfstan,
Archbishop of Jorvik (from our side), and the
Archbishop of Canterbury (from the Saxon side)
called a truce before any of us got our swords
dirty.

Erik's moaning about "spoilsports." He says
what's the point of winning if you haven't actually
fought?

Personally, I don't mind not fighting. I'd like to
live to be an old man.

Edmund became King of the Saxons when Athelstan died.

Jorvik

I've been talking to Archbishop Wulfstan. He's a clever old goat. A lot of priests aren't interested in anything that happens outside their church's walls. Wulfstan's different. He has more political clout than almost anyone else in Jorvik. It was his idea to invite Olaf to be king. He's been trying to explain the political situation to me. It's very complicated:

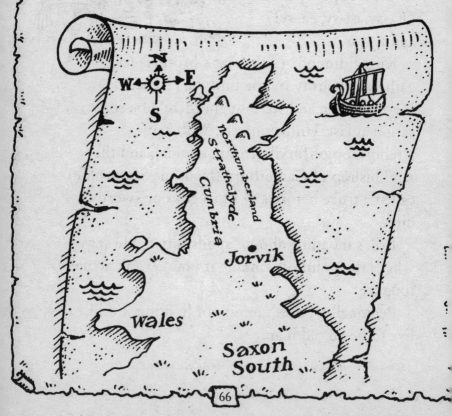

The Cumbrians and the Strathclyde Welsh are pretty quiet at the moment, but there could be trouble for us if the Northumbrians team up with the Saxons in the South.

Wulfstan said that in a week things could change. Kingdoms come and go, and borders keep shifting. Sometimes you get someone to draw you a map, and it's out of date before the ink's dry.

I tried to explain all this to Erik. He listened for a while, but then he got that glazed look that comes over his face when anybody tries to tell him anything more complicated than what's for breakfast.

"Well, Gorblime," he said, "if things change that fast, it's a waste of time trying to understand them."

Vikings aren't very good at politics. They just enjoy hitting people and taking things.

I like Jorvik. You never know who you're going to run into. There are all kinds of people here—lots of Danes, of course, but also Vikings from Norway, Sweden, and Iceland; Frisians from the Low Countries; Britons—you name it. Just yesterday I had lunch with Bjorn-To Run (Swedish), Magnus Mägazinräk (Icelandic),

Makehay Van Der Sunshines (Dutch), Hows Itgoingsson (Norwegian), and Bill Smith (don't Britons have funny names?).

Bad news arrived this morning.

We haven't heard much about Erik's old enemy, Egil Skallagrimson, recently. He's been lying low in Iceland. But he's back now, and he's really gone overboard this time!

Ever since the Gula Assembly, he's been waiting for an opportunity to get back at Onund (who got Egil's wife's inheritance after Gunnhild's brother smashed up the court). Egil also had it in for Erik and Gunnhild, and he wanted to teach them a lesson.

Erik's son Rognvald was staying with Onund. Egil and his men attacked during the night and slaughtered everyone. Poor Rognvald was only ten years old.

Afterward, Egil made up a poem boasting about what he'd done:

> *Bloodaxe's debt has been paid,*
> *His boy is with Odin*
> *To Gunnhild's grief...*

The whole kingdom went into mourning, and Gunnhild was inconsolable. She locked herself in her room for days and refused to eat.

Erik went berserk. He swore on his own life that he would track Egil down and make him regret what he'd done.

Egil had better stay out of Erik's way from now on!

Jorvik

Poor old King Olaf Guthfrithson, King of Dublin and Jorvik, died today.

It's not right for a Viking chieftain to die in his bed. It means he will go to Niflheim, the land of eternal ice, ruled by Hel, the Queen of the Dead. A Viking who dies in battle goes to the gods' country, Asgard. Every day he fights again in the greatest of all battles, and every evening he goes to feast with Odin, the father of the gods, in Valhalla, the Hall of the Slain. Valhalla has walls made of golden spears and a roof made of golden shields.

It has five hundred and forty doors, each wide enough to allow eight hundred men to pass through side by side. Every night, the hall is filled with Viking warriors eating and drinking to their heart's content. (Gunnhild says she doesn't know whose job it is to clean up the mess, but she's glad it isn't hers.)

The new King of Jorvik is Cuaran. I don't like him. A real Viking will spear you through the chest (that's fair play), but Cuaran will stab you in the back and then claim someone else did it.

Erik said this to Earl Orm while they were taking a break down at the Plunder and Pillage meadhouse. Orm's a decent old geezer; he helped Olaf Guthfrithson plan the Danelaw campaign and let him marry his daughter. He's also a member of the Witan*. He told Erik he didn't like Cuaran much either, but the Witan had chosen him, so that was that.

It's pretty obvious why the Witan chose Cuaran. The Saxons have resolved their squabbles and are growing stronger again. If there's a strong king in Jorvik, the Saxons might not attack. So creepy Cuaran has been chosen to keep the Saxons quiet.

* The Witan—the governing council of Jorvik

I'm getting used to living in Jorvik, although it felt very crowded at first. There are more than 30,000 people here. Most of them live inside the city walls, but there's not enough room for everyone. More houses are built along some of the roads leading out of the city.

The roads are very muddy a lot of the time, so most trade is carried by boats.

The Vikings all live in a part of the city that's south of the old Roman citadel.

The houses are longhouses made of wattle and daub with thatched roofs, just like the ones back home only smaller. But instead of one longhouse there are many, all built facing each other across wooden walkways. It's very civilized.

I said this to Gunnhild (who arrived from the Orkneys last week), and she gave me an earful. "That's Vikings for you," she raged. "A thousand years ago the Romans were building cities of stone, and you think it's sophisticated to live in a hut with a grass roof and walls made out of sticks, mud, and cow-dung!"

Gunnhild can say what she likes, but Jorvik's not a bad place, for a city. There are lots of alehouses, and you can usually find a good fight (or start one), but I like the wide-open spaces of Norway better. I think I must be pining for the fjords.

Jorvik

In the spring, news came that the Saxons had retaken the Danelaw. If Olaf Guthfrithson were alive, he'd have sent his men down there to give the Saxons a good beating—but King Cuaran isn't doing anything! Old Earl Orm just shakes his head and says it can't be helped, but Archbishop Wulfstan is in a rage. I'm not a Christian so I don't go to church, but apparently Wulfstan has been preaching sermons against the Saxons that would make your hair stand on end.

Erik's decided we should do some raiding around Northumbria and Scotland, just to keep in practice. I haven't been raiding for months, but I suppose it's like driving an oxcart—once you've learned, you never forget.

Northumbria

Erik asked me to write a special praise song for the men to sing while they're rowing.

Hi ho, hi ho,
A-Viking we will go.
With an axe and sword,
We're never bored.
Hi ho, hi ho, hi ho.
(REPEAT AT LEAST 100 TIMES)

It's not a bad song, and you can either whistle it or sing it. We sang it all over Northumbria and Scotland. It was great until the novelty wore off.

The NORSE of the WORLD

RAGNALD
ALL THE RAGE!

Ragnald Guthfrithson is now the new King of Jorvik after having sensationally booted out Cuaran. Ragnald, the brother of the dead ex-King of Jorvik, Olaf Guthfrithson, is a popular choice as king and has promised to stand up to the Saxons.

Erik Bloodaxe, who has recently returned from a successful raiding season, was very happy about the new appointment: "At least we might get some action against the Saxon swine now that loser Cuaran is out. I'm tickled pink and looking forward to seeing a lot of violence very soon."

Ragnald is certainly no wimp like Cuaran. So it's no more Mr. Nice-guy. Watch out, you Saxons, here we come!

SUPER NORSE OF THE WORLD BINGO See p. 4

Jorvik

Erik and I visited old Earl Orm to find out what he
thought about Ragnald taking over. Archbishop
Wulfstan was with him, so we had a bite to eat and
started talking about religion.

Erik told Wulfstan all about Odin, the father of the
gods, and Thor, the god of thunder; about the
goddesses, Frigg and Freyja, and Loki, the god of
tricks and mischief; of Balder the Bright, Idunn who
keeps the apples of youth, and Mimir whose head
was struck off yet who continues to teach the gods
wisdom. He spoke of Asgard, the land of the gods,
and Midgard, the land of men; of the first man, Ask,
and the first woman, Embla; of Kvasir, the wisest of
all men, and the Norns, who know each man's
destiny; of the dwarves and dark elves who live
beneath the earth, and the serpent, Jormungand, who
lies in a circle around the Earth biting his own tail,
beneath the sea where Aegir and Ran rule. He told
Wulfstan of Hel, Queen of the Dead, and Garm, who
guards the gates of the Underworld. And he spoke of
the great ash tree, Yggdrasil, which holds all the
worlds in place; and of Fenrir the wolf, whose coming
signals Ragnarok, the end of the world.

Thor

Idunn

Embla

Then Erik asked Wulfstan how many gods the Christians had, and he said "one." Erik didn't believe him at first. He said it couldn't be much of a religion with only one god.

Wulfstan said the Christian God was a very powerful god.

Erik said, "He'd have to be."

Wulfstan said the Christian God knew everything, but I think that was just boasting. Even Odin doesn't know everything, not even after he gave up one of his eyes for a drink from the fountain of knowledge.

Wulfstan asked Erik what he believed would

Balder the Bright

Loki

happen to him after he was dead, and Erik told him all about Valhalla and the fighting and the feasting and so on. Then he asked Wulfstan what happened to Christians when they died, and Wulfstan told him about heaven and hell. He said you went to hell if you were wicked, and demons tortured you in flame for all eternity; but if you were good you went to heaven and sang with the angels and sat around on clouds playing the harp all day long forever.

Erik said he thought hell sounded like more fun. Either way, he said, it didn't sound like much of an afterlife to *him*.

AD 944

Jorvik

Everybody's very nervous. Rumors are flying that the Saxons are preparing for war and that King Edmund is planning to invade Jorvik. The Witan is having kittens.

If you ask me, King Ragnald has become a Christian to try to show the Saxons he's trustworthy (fat chance!).

Ragnald was telling Erik about his conversion the other day. "Jesus saves," he said.

"Really?" said Erik. "Where does he keep his money?"

King Ragnald explained that that wasn't what he meant, but Erik wasn't convinced. He knows churches always have plenty of money; that's why he raids so many.

The NORSE of the WORLD

GOOD TO BE BACK!

CUARAN IN, RAGNALD OUT

In, out, in, out, and shake it all about!

Kings have been doing the hökey-pökey this week! Yesterday, ex-King Cuaran returned to Jorvik with a mighty Saxon army that booted Ragnald out and set Cuaran on the throne of Jorvik for the second time!

Like Ragnald, Cuaran has recently converted to Christianity, which is dismal news for all the Odin-worshipping Vikings in Jorvik. No more partying or pillaging! It's down-on-your-knees-and-pray-for-your-soul time!

The NORSE OF THE WORLD says "Amen" to that!

Welcome back, Your Kingship!

Next Week: Riches to Rags!

My Tragic Story by Ex-King Ragnald,
Only in the Norse of the World.

Erik can't wait to get out of Jorvik. There's not enough fighting and feasting for his liking. Also, there's a rumor that the Saxon King, Edmund, can't stand Ragnald or Cuaran and plans to take Jorvik over himself.

We can't stop him, so it's back to the Orkneys for Erik.

The Orkney Islands

Things are pretty quiet these days. Vikings control most of the islands around Scotland, the Orkneys, the Hebrides, and most of the West Coast. The countryside is gorgeous, but you can't eat scenery—and most of the Viking settlements are well defended against raids.

So we're passing the time farming and trading, with some raiding here and there for fun. Gunnhild grumbles constantly that she married the King of Norway, not a sheep farmer. Why isn't Erik trying to get his throne back? The answer to that, as she well knows, is that it's a waste of time. The Vikings in Norway actually like Hakon (they call him Hakon the Good) because he stays out of their way.

So Gunnhild sulks a lot. In between sulks, she's got her sons to raise. Erik has five sons now. The eldest, Harald, is turning out to be a fighter like his father.

AD 946

The Orkney Islands

I'm bored with the day-to-day lifestyle on the island. I wrote a song about it to sing to Erik at the next feast—he's just as bored as I am.

ORKNEY RAP
Well, I woke up this mornin', got outta my bed,
Pulled my linen shirt right over my head,
Put on linen pants and woolen britches,
And then my blue tunic with the yellow stitches.
Now Gunnhild says I look like a fool,
But in the snow I feel real cool.
The life is hard, the life is crude,
It ain't no place for a real cool dude
In the Orkneys.

I go to the fields to bring in the hay,
I feel like I'm throwing my life away.
I practice swordplay hour after hour;
If you wanna survive, you gotta get power!
I go to the court, got a case to bring,
(I like to call that doin' my "Thing")

The feast each night goes on 'til three,
But the food is tough, and it sickens me
In the Orkneys.

I wanna raid, I wanna fight!
Just sittin' around, it don't seem right.
I need a ship, the seas to roam
A Viking's place ain't in the home.
I'll tell you once, I'll tell you twice,
Now you all listen to my advice,
Don't ever come over here to live
We sure ain't got nothing to give
In the Orkneys.

This song has an unusual beat. I think I'll call it
hip höp.

AD 947

The Orkney Islands

One or two of the Jorvik Vikings have joined us
recently. Apparently things are pretty bad in
Jorvik. King Edmund died last year, but his son,
Eadred, booted King Cuaran out and called the
Jorvik government together a few months ago. He
told the Witan that he was the new King of England,
and that included Jorvik, so he didn't want anybody
getting any ideas. Archbishop Wulfstan and Earl
Orm had no choice but to say, "Right, Chief," but
if I know wily old Wulfstan, he's just waiting for
Eadred to drop his guard. When he does, the
Saxons had better watch out.

Gunnhild's complaining continues. Choose any of
the following. You can bet she'll be whining about
it.

> It's cold.

> There aren't
> any stores.

> It's boring.

> It's still boring.

> She preferred
> being a queen.

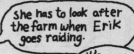

She has to look after the farm when Erik goes raiding.

She has to look after the kids when Erik goes raiding.

It's even more boring.

She keeps trying to persuade Erik to go back to Jorvik, but Erik won't budge. Gunnhild says at least Jorvik is a civilized place with stores and real houses and polite society, not like this wretched island where she's surrounded by barbarians and goat droppings.

Erik holds his ground and says he won't be ruled by a Saxon king. This puts Gunnhild into a major sulk, so Erik goes off on a raid to get out of the way. Then she starts griping all over again.

I can see Erik's point. Some of the Saxons are decent people, but would you let your daughter marry one?

Erik says he's not going back to Jorvik, not now, not ever. Wild horses couldn't drag him near the place. He swears on his mother's life, on Odin's good eye, and on his own name that nothing on Earth will ever persuade him to set foot in Jorvik again.

THE NORSE of the WORLD

THE AXE IS BACK!

Erik Bloodaxe is back in Jorvik, and this time he's back as KING!

After years of being pushed around by the Saxons, Archbishop Wulfstan and Earl Orm sent a message to Erik:

"Come and be king and bring back the great days of Olaf Guthfrithson!"

Luckily for Jorvik, Erik said, "YES, YES, YES!!!" *Actually, Gunnhild said yes, yes, yes.* Beefy King Erik has all the right credentials:

- he's a warrior
- he's got a lovely wife AND
- he's been a king before! Asked if he had a message for the Saxons, Erik said: "Watch out you no good Sax, 'Cause I'm after you with my Blood axe!"

King Eadred of the Saxons was unavailable *I had to make up this rhyme on the spot — not one of my better ones.* for comment this morning, but a spokesman for the palace said that the King was fully informed of the situation. It seems from this that Eadred doesn't like the idea of tangling with Big Erik.

The NORSE OF THE WORLD says "Welcome back, Axe!"

WIN an ERIk BLoodaxe Axe See p. 12

FIRST AID TIPS: Axe wounds with DR. FINLAYSSON See p. 9

AD 948

Jorvik

Gunnhild is happy now; she hated not being queen. I think Erik's determined to hold on to his kingdom this time. The first thing he did was to send for Aethelferth and Rathulf, the people who make money, and have them make new coins with his name on them. The coins say "Erik Rex." I think that makes him sound like a dog, but Wulfstan tells me that *Rex* is Latin for King. Erik doesn't care; he just likes spending coins with his picture on them.

However, there's a catch to all this "Please-be-our-king-we-think-you're-so-great" business. Wulfstan says Erik has to become a Christian before he can be crowned king.

Erik got quite stubborn about that and says he's not going to become a Christian—not now, not ever. Wild horses couldn't drag him near a church. He swears on his mother's life, on Odin's good eye, and on his own name that nothing on Earth will ever persuade him to become a Christian.

THE NORSE OF THE WORLD

ERIK CONVERTS!

Gunnhild hit him with a rolling pin →

King Erik Bloodaxe has become a Christian! Some people say the only reason he has done this is to become king. Erik himself denies this.

"I deny this," he told our reporter. "I have in fact recently had a deeply religious experience. Therefore I have decided to convert to the only true religion. I now believe in heaven and hell."

Full Coverage of King Erik's Coronation
See p. 2

Jorvik

Guess who showed up at court today? Your enemy and mine, Egil Skallagrimson!

It seems Egil got shipwrecked at the mouth of the Humber River. When he realized that he'd landed in Erik's country, he decided there was no chance of escaping from him, so instead of hiding he's come to Jorvik. I must admit, the man has guts.

I went to Egil's cell to see him. He asked me what I thought Erik would do to him. I pointed out one or two of Egil's misdemeanors that Erik might be a little unhappy about:

1) He'd always been Erik's enemy.
2) He'd insulted Erik.
3) He'd killed several of Erik and Gunnhild's best friends.
4) He'd killed one of Erik's sons.

The chances were that Egil wouldn't get off with just a slap on the wrist.

Egil asked if there was anything he could do to get on Erik's good side. I told him to compose a praise song in twenty verses. If Erik liked it, he might just let him off. (No chance!)

Egil wasn't happy, but he didn't really have any choice.

At court this morning, Egil asked King Erik to forgive him, or at least let him go free. Gunnhild said he must be kidding. Now that Erik had Egil where he wanted him, the only question was whether Egil wanted to be buried in the ground or at sea.

Egil said he had spent the night composing a praise song for Erik.

"Go ahead, let's hear it. I bet it's terrible," said Erik.

Egil cleared his throat and began.

"Erik isn't so bad, really..."

There was a swishing sound as Erik's men drew their swords.

Egil licked his lips and went on, "I mean,

Erik is a great guy. Honest."

Erik's men stepped forward, fingering the edges of their swords in a threatening manner.

Egil closed his eyes and, from some secret well of terror, began his praise song.

Swordmetal shone,
Shields shattered.
Death danced abroad
On that fell field;
Carrion crows gathered
To feast on the fallen.
Scots lay asleep,
Never to waken;
Wages for wolves,
Rewards for the raven.
Amid fallen foes
The sea wolf sings;
Erik the mighty,
Greatest of Kings!

And so on. There was a lot more of the same. It was the best praise song I'd ever heard. It just goes to show what you can do if you're under pressure.

When he'd finished, Erik nodded and said, "Not bad." Gunnhild looked at him in astonishment. Surely he wasn't going to . . .

Erik silenced her with a gesture (he is a king after all) and looked Egil straight in the eye.

"Just don't let me see you again," he said. "Ever. I mean it."

Egil didn't hang around.

You might think it's strange that Erik let his son's murderer go free just because he made up a flattering poem about him. But that's Vikings for you. A good praise song can spread your fame around the whole world, and to a Viking, fame is everything. Egil wouldn't have gotten away by offering Erik money or land . . . but immortality is a great gift.

In fact, in a thousand years, somebody might read that poem of Egil's in a book, and Erik's fame will go on. Isn't that worth a man's life?

But Erik's not stupid. He also made Egil give him all his money.

Jorvik

There's trouble brewing. I didn't expect King Eadred of England to be too happy about Erik being King of Jorvik, and he isn't. He's gathered a Saxon army, and he's coming up the Great North Road like a wolf after a fat pig. Just to show that he's in a fighting mood, he's burning every town and fort along the way and slaughtering opposition. Some members of the Witan are beginning to get nervous.

THE NORSE OF THE WORLD

SAXONS LET RIP ON RIPON

The murderous Saxon army has destroyed Ripon!

Reports say that they ruthlessly attacked the city. The three hundred people living there were put to the sword (and the spear, the arrow, and the axe).

BURNT OFFERINGS

The Saxons also burned down the Cathedral of St. Wilfrid, and the Archbishop of Canterbury has stolen all the cathedral's relics and taken them to Kent "for safe-keeping."

Archbishop Wulfstan is absolutely furious that the Saxons have stolen holy relics belonging to Jorvik. "I'm absolutely furious," he confirmed.

He is urging Erik to attack the Saxons immediately. "Go after the Saxons and kill every one of them."

PULL BACK

It is also reported that the Saxons are ashamed of what they have done and are starting to pull back south without attacking Jorvik.

Inside reports indicate they are trying to negotiate a peace, stating that if Erik leaves them alone, they'll leave Jorvik alone. This approach is supported by namby-pamby Earl Orm.

However, the NORSE OF THE WORLD is with Wulfstan, and we say, "Go get 'em, Erik!"

CARTOONS: New Strip Starts Today!
Pnuts and Snööpi See p. 11

97

Jorvik

Erik ambushed the Saxon rear guard as they were trying to cross the Aire River at Castleford, and he wiped them out.

Wulfstan is dancing for joy, and the city's full of cheering crowds. But Orm's looking gloomier than ever. He says the Saxons haven't been defeated in open battle for nearly fifty years, and Eadred will be breathing fire.

No good will come of this, mark my words.

Jorvik

YIKES! We could be up to our necks in trouble! Eadred's turned right around again and is heading back north with fresh troops. Those

members of the Witan who were cheering loudest when they heard Erik had routed the Saxons are now muttering that their king has been "hot-blooded" and "too hasty."

Erik, ignoring the warning signs, is ready for more fighting. As far as he's concerned, the more Saxons we have to fight the merrier. Ha!

The Witan doesn't see it like that. Rumor has it they're secretly sending gifts and ambassadors to Eadred. My guess is they want to make peace with Eadred before he attacks, and if the price of that peace is getting rid of Erik, then that's what they'll do.

THE NORSE OF THE WORLD

HOW ZAT?!

ERIK OUT! CUARAN IN! (AGAIN!)

Erik Bloodaxe has been dumped! After only a year as king he's been told to pack his bags and hit the road!

This decision was reached by the Jorvik Witan after a meeting yesterday. It was prompted by King Eadred, who promised not to attack Jorvik if the Witan agreed to his two demands:

1) to banish Erik.
2) to make Cuaran king for the third time!

It is reported that Wulfstan strode around the Witan telling them they were all cowards, but when the votes were counted, it was bye-bye, Erik.

Hello again, King Cuaran!

This Week's Recipe:
King Cuaran Cake with Martha Stewartsson
See the Food Page

Jorvik

Gunnhild isn't speaking to Erik; in fact, she's not speaking to anybody (if you don't count her constant muttering under her breath, things like "Great pudding-headed, jelly-brained lump of cow dung" whenever Erik's name is mentioned).

If you ask me, Jorvik is getting what it deserves. If they're not tough enough to have a real Viking in charge, they deserve Cuaran, who's nothing more than Eadred's puppet.

As for us? Back to the Orkneys!

AD 949

The Orkney Islands

It's winter in the Orkneys again, and we're all
freezing! The sun comes up for about ten minutes
at lunchtime—unless it's cloudy, which it usually
is. There's nothing to do except hunt seals and
walruses.

Living here is like watching seaweed grow.

We were just getting ready for the new raiding
season when several longships showed up at our
settlement. We thought they'd come to attack us,
so we grabbed our weapons, but it turned out
they just wanted to talk to Erik.

They want to start a Kingdom of the Hebrides
for all the Vikings who live around the coasts and
islands from the west to the north of Scotland.
Since Erik was the only genuine unemployed

royal among them, they asked him to be king. Of course, Erik said yes. Being King of the Hebrides is kind of a letdown after being King of Jorvik, but it's better than a slap in the face with a wet herring. A kingdom is a kingdom after all. It has also cheered Gunnhild up because she gets to be a queen again!

So we killed a few goats and got out some barrels of Gunnhild's home-brewed ale and had a feast.

The Hebrides Vikings turned out to be a good bunch of guys, and we were soon singing old Viking songs:

> *A-Viking, A-Viking*
> *A-Viking's been my ru-i-ning!*
> *I'll go no more A-Vi-i-king*
> *With you, fair maid!*

And:

> *Oh, you take the high tide, and I'll*
> *   take the low tide,*
> *And I'll be in Scotland afore ye!*
> *We'll sail into the bay and we'll make*
> *   the Scotsmen pay,*
> *On the bonny bonny banks of*
> *   Glen Goolie!*

AD 950

The Orkney Islands

We picked up quite a few slaves in the raids this summer, but we can't keep them over the winter, because there's not enough food to go around. Of course, we sold all the warriors we'd captured back to their families and friends for ransom, so all we have left is poor slaves whose families can't afford to buy them back. We were racking our brains trying to decide what to do with them when I had an idea.

"Why don't we sell them to the Moors?" I said.

"Who are the Moors?" said Erik.

I had to explain that Moors were Arabs who came from North Africa, but they'd taken over Spain too.

"I've heard from Viking traders that the Moors are looking for slaves," I told Erik. "What's more, we'd have to deliver them to Spain."

Gunnhild's eyes lit up. "We could take a vacation!" she cried.

So that was decided.

Atlantic Ocean

We set out for Spain this morning. Even Gunnhild joined in the rowing song:

> *Oh, we're sailing off to sunny Spain.*
> *Viva España!*
> *We are rowing south with might and main.*
> *Viva España!*
> *Though the Spanish don't speak any Norse –*
> *(They can't understañ' ya)*
> *We'll sell our slaves off to the Moors.*
> *España! Por favor!*

Everybody's enjoying themselves, except the slaves, who are crying and being seasick. You just can't please some people.

Spain

We were able to sell most of our slaves right away, so now we're lazing around on the beach drinking some strange mead made out of grapes. It's not bad, which is more than I can say for Spanish cooking. I don't like eating spicy food. And they smother everything in olive oil. Give me rancid walrus drippings any day.

Spain

We set sail for home today. Most of the men have bought little toy donkeys with straw hats. Of course, I didn't buy anything as cheap and tacky as that. I've got a bullfight poster with my name on it. Olé.

Famous Matador.
Gorblime Leifitoutsson

AD 951

Spain

When we got back to the Orkneys, Gunnhild
kept whining that she wanted to go back to Spain
because she liked the weather. So this year we
picked up a lot of Britons, Saxons, Scots, and Irish
in the spring raids, and here we are in Spain again
to sell them to the Moors.

There's some competition this year from
Vikings selling captives from their wars with
Eastern European people called Slavs. (In fact, a
slave trader told me the other day that the word
"slave" comes from the word "Slav" because the
Vikings have sold so many of their Slav captives
to the Arabs. Not many people know that!)

North Africa

Trade was slow in Spain, so we're trying our luck in North Africa. It's really hot here. The sun burns down out of a cloudless sky, and the heat rises off the sand in ripples that look like the waves of the sea. If it gets any warmer I'll have to take my helmet off.

I've never seen a country like this. People ride strange animals called camels. One of the locals told me that camels don't need to eat or drink too often, which is a good thing since they live in the desert. When the weather is very hot, these huge beasts can drink up to fifty-three gallons (two hundred liters) of water a day! I had my doubts about this, so I asked where the camel puts all that liquid. The man told me that the animals store much of the water in the large humps on their backs. The humps are made up mostly of fat. When a camel is traveling across the hot, dry desert, it gets much of its energy from the fat and water in its hump.

The Moors in Africa seem very interested in learning (something we Vikings don't care all that much about). Many people know how to read and write. I hope none of them try to convince Erik that they're better poets than me. It would be just my luck to get stuck in this awful place for the rest of my life. I'd better write a few praise poems to keep on his good side.

The Orkney Islands

When I saw the paper this morning, my eyes nearly bugged out. I tried to hide it, but Erik came in and made me read it to him:

The NORSE of the WORLd

BRING BACK ERIK

King Olaf Cuaran was booted out of the Kingdom of Jorvik last night by angry Vikings. Cuaran's third reign ended when a mob stormed the palace.

PLUNDER BLUNDER
The crowd chanted, "We want plunder!" as they raided Cuaran's headquarters. Vikings in Jorvik are upset because Cuaran has told them not to go on raids. Archbishop Wulfstan, who has been demanding Cuaran's resignation for years, told our reporter, "Cuaran's had his chance. It's time we had a real king again. Bring back Erik!" This cry was taken up by the crowd.

Will Erik Return?
See p. 5

Spot the Battleaxe Competition –
Thousands of Slaves to be won!
See pp. 10-11

Before I'd gotten to the end of the first page, Erik had rushed off to pack and Gunnhild was dusting off her crown.

It's all going to go badly wrong again, I just know it!

Jorvik

When we got to Jorvik, Earl Orm met us. He looked worried. He told us he was sorry Wulfstan wasn't there to meet us: he'd been invited to pay a visit to King Eadred of the Saxons but had promised to be back for Erik's return. In spite of this, he hadn't come back, and Earl Orm was concerned that he'd been arrested.

There's nothing we can do about Wulfstan now, so Erik's busy moving into the palace, which is built around the old Roman gatehouse. It's like an ordinary longhouse but much bigger. Gunnhild always complains that Erik shouldn't let people build their houses right up to the walls of his palace, but Erik says a Viking can build wherever he wants to.

💀⚔️💀⚔️💀⚔️💀⚔️💀

We've received news of Wulfstan at last, but it isn't good! Eadred has him locked up in an old Roman fort in Essex. Erik was ready to go down there to rescue him, but Orm says the place is surrounded by marsh and has walls thirteen feet (four meters) thick, so forget it. This is worrisome. King Erik is a fine Viking warrior, which means he's good at chopping people to pieces, but he's not good on strategy: brave as a lion but not too bright. I don't know how long he'll stay king without Wulfstan to advise him.

The NORSE of the WORLD

HERE COMES THE TARTAN ARMY

EXCLUSIVE

The NORSE of the WORLD has learned that an army is on its way down from the North to attack Jorvik and drive King Erik out.

This army is an alliance of:
- Northumbrians
- Scots
- Cumbrians

Its leader is King Indulf of Scotland, but since "Windy Indy" has been king for only a couple of weeks, the attack may not be his idea. Oswulf, Earl of Bamburgh, is reported to be behind the whole thing. The ambitious Oswulf has a lot to gain. If he can add Jorvik to Northumbria, he hopes to set up a northern Saxon kingdom to rival that of King Eadred in the South.

King Erik is in a feisty mood. He has stated that it doesn't matter whose idea it is, if Indulf and Oswulf want a fight they can have one.

The NORSE of the WORLD says, "GO, ERIK, SHOW 'EM WHO'S KING!"

Jorvik

I'll say this for Erik, when it comes to fighting he doesn't kid around. He's really determined to stay king this time!

It wasn't a very long battle. Most of the enemy took one look at Erik's face and decided they'd rather be somewhere else. Time for another praise song:

Fear filled our foes; fight left them.
Sick at heart, they sighed and shook;
Few escaped the wrath of Erik.
Tears were shed by many mothers...

We were still celebrating our victory when a messenger arrived from Oswulf, Earl of Bamburgh. Since we'd only just finished wiping out his army, it seemed strange that Oswulf should want to pay a visit, but Erik agreed to see him.

Oswulf showed up the next day. He blamed Indulf for the attack on Jorvik and said he'd come on behalf of the people of Northumbria to swear loyalty to Erik. Erik was pleased as punch, but I can't say I was. Oswulf looks like a smooth talker, and I wouldn't trust him as far as I could throw a longship.

Orm doesn't trust him either and tried to warn Erik to be careful, but Erik believes in the Viking code of honor (it's called the Norse code). He respects his enemies, and he expects them to respect him. I don't think Earl Oswulf would know what honor was if it bit him on the backside.

AD 953

Jorvik

Erik's just had an argument with Earl Orm. The old earl keeps trying to warn him about Oswulf, but Erik won't listen. He told Orm he was a crazy old fool, and Orm said he'd had enough insults from Erik and stormed off.

WHAT AN IDIOT

YOU CRAZY OLD FOOL

WHAT A DOPE

Slimy Oswulf has Erik just where he wants him. Gunnhild likes the man, too, and so do the members of the Witan, but if I ever saw a guy up to no good, it's Oswulf.

People are upset that Wulfstan hasn't come back. The Church is very important in Jorvik; in fact, there are ten churches besides the Church of St. Peter, which is Wulfstan's cathedral. The people are getting nervous because it's Wulfstan's job to give bread to the poor when times are hard. They worry that if Wulfstan doesn't come back, no one will feed them.

Erik mentioned this to Oswulf, who tut-tutted and said he'd try to think of something. Whatever he comes up with, it won't be to Erik's advantage, you can bet on that.

AD 954

Jorvik

Erik's packing to go an a pilgrimage! This is all Oswulf's idea. He told Erik that if he visited the shrine of St. Cuthbert (which is miles away at Cuncacestir*) he would show the people of Jorvik and Northumberland that he was a proper Christian king who'd take care of them. Then they'd stop worrying about Wulfstan.

When Erik told old Orm this, he went ballistic. I made a note of what they each said in the calm, sensible debate that followed:

*Cuncacestir – Chester-le-Street

After this frank exchange of views, Orm went off in a sulk and Erik told Oswulf he'd visit St. Cuthbert.

I don't know what the world's coming to. The greatest Viking warrior of the age is going off to see some moldy old saint. There'll be trouble before this is over with.

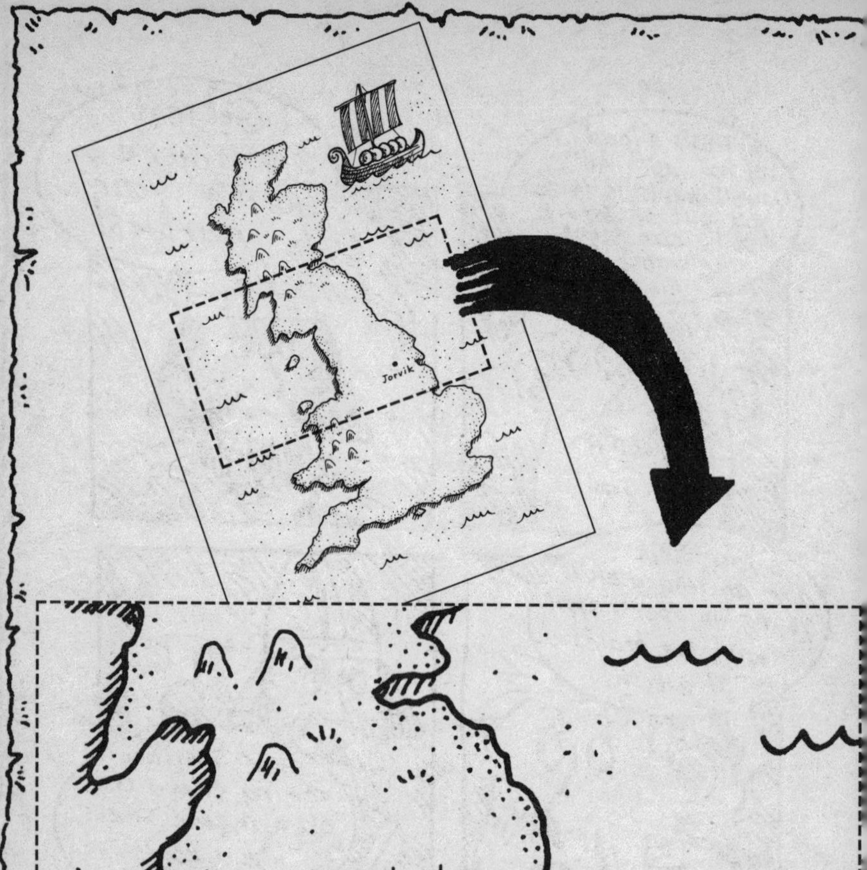

Hagustaldesea

Luel

Cuncacestir

Steinmore Jorvik

Cuncacestir

We arrived at the shrine of St. Cuthbert this afternoon. Oswulf had told Erik the saint would be really pleased to get a gift, so Erik had his coffin opened (something I'd never do) and put an arm-ring and piece of silk inside. I don't know if St. Cuthbert was pleased; he was certainly grinning, but then, most skeletons do.

Near Cuncacestir

We'd just started back to Jorvik when a messenger arrived. It wasn't good news. As soon as Erik's back was turned, Oswulf announced that he was taking over and that Erik was exiled again. Even Gunnhild couldn't complain this time, because she's always told Erik to listen to Oswulf's advice. She said, "Ah, well, there's always the Hebrides."

I expected Erik to go crazy, but not this time. He got very quiet and said he'd been kicked out of his kingdom twice before and he wasn't going to let it happen again. He told Gunnhild to head back to the Orkneys. She would have to raise Erik's sons if anything happened to him.

Then Erik turned south and set off back to Jorvik.

Hagustaldesea

We got word that Oswulf's entire army was waiting for us on the road to the south, so we turned back and headed along the old Roman wall to Luel. We're going to cross the Pennines and go around behind Oswulf's men while they're looking the other way.

Steinmore

I'm writing this before I get too weak to finish
Erik's story.

Oswulf's men ambushed us as we were crossing
Steinmore. Erik fought bravely. Surrounded by
his enemies, he shouted for reinforcements.
"A Norse! A Norse! My kingdom for a Norse!"
he cried, but no help came. On that cold, bleak
moor, Erik was cut down along with his son
Haeric and his guards.

I was badly wounded but managed to escape.

The people who have taken me in say that it was Oswulf's son, Earl Maccus, who killed Erik. I would write more, but I feel my life is slipping away. Like my master, Erik, I shall die a Viking's death, and I know that on the other side of the darkness Valhalla awaits me.

I wonder if they've got a job opening for a really good poet?

HISTORICAL NOTE: BY R. CELAVIE, PROFESSOR OF HISTORY

University of Hard Knocks, Peoria

Although all the facts contained in this diary and the newspaper clippings are more or less correct, there are several mistakes that lead me to believe that this "diary" is a clever forgery.

It must be admitted that the story told here fits all the known facts, and that the picture of York (Jorvik) in the tenth century is largely accurate. Erik Bloodaxe really was the King of Norway and of York.

However:

- There was certainly never a Viking newspaper called *The Norse of the World*.

- The map on pages 26 and 27 shows fjords, provinces, and towns that never existed, although Oslofjord, Tonsberg, Trondheim, and the Island of Atley are correctly identified.

- The "original" journal is written in runes dating from the thirteenth century. There is no evidence that vellum (cured animal hide) was used in the tenth century. (It is possible that the hides allegedly found in the Steinmore burial mound are copies of original runes carved on stone or wood, but this seems unlikely.)

- Though Egil Skallagrimson's story is told in Egil's saga, no Viking saga mentions a Viking poet called Gorblime Leifitoutsson, and it seems obvious he is a completely fictitious character.

It's clear to me that the so-called writers, Barlow and Skidmore, have committed a clever fraud. If you see them, call the authorities immediately!

THE END OF ERIK'S STORY: Erik Bloodaxe was the last Viking King of Jorvik. After his death, the Saxon King Eadred took power, and the Kingdom of Jorvik came to an end. Erik's widow, Queen Gunnhild, reached the Orkneys safely and later went to her brother Harald's court in Denmark. There she plotted against Hakon, who had taken the throne of Norway from Erik. The son of Erik and Gunnhild, Harald Graycloak, completed her revenge by killing Hakon in AD 960 and became King of Norway. After Erik's death, Archbishop Wulfstan was set free, but he was never allowed to return to Jorvik. He was made Bishop of Dorchester and died there in AD 956.